D1162041

Grumpy Bear

Best Friend Bear

This book belongs to: _____

Secret Bear

Wish Bear

Love-a-lot Bear

Care Bears™ © 2006 Those Characters From Cleveland, Inc.
Used under license by Scholastic Inc. All rights reserved.

No part of this publication may be reproduced in whole or in part, or stored in a retrieval system,
or transmitted in any form or by any means, electronic, mechanical, photocopying, recording, or
otherwise, without written permission of the publisher. For information regarding permission,
write to: Scholastic Inc., Attention: Permissions Department, 557 Broadway, New York, NY 10012.

Published by Scholastic Inc.
90 Old Sherman Turnpike, Danbury, CT 06816.

SCHOLASTIC and associated logos are trademarks and/or registered trademarks of Scholastic Inc.

ISBN 0-439-83580-1

First Scholastic Printing, March 2006

Care Bears™ Friendship Club

Look for the Silver Lining

by Frances Ann Ladd
& Quinlan B. Lee

Illustrated by
Jay Johnson &
Warner McGee

SCHOLASTIC INC.

New York   Toronto   London   Auckland   Sydney
Mexico City   New Delhi   Hong Kong   Buenos Aires

Secret Bear found Grumpy Bear
looking a little blue.
"What's wrong?" she asked him.
"Can you tell me or is it
a secret?"

"I'm just feeling grumpy today," he replied. "That's all."

"I know just the thing to cheer you up— a picnic!" Secret Bear said.

"Okay," said Grumpy Bear, smiling just a bit.

Secret Bear and Grumpy Bear hurried
to invite their friends to a picnic.

"That sounds cheerific!"

said Cheer Bear. "I'll bring my picnic blanket."

"Uh-oh," Cheer Bear said.
"I can't find my picnic blanket anywhere."

"See," said Grumpy Bear.
"Something's going wrong
already."

"Don't worry," Secret Bear replied. "It's sure to turn up somewhere."

Just then a **big fat** raindrop plopped
onto Grumpy Bear's nose.

"Now the rain's going to spoil
everything," he cried.

"This is a terrible day for a picnic."

13

"No worries,"
said Cheer Bear. "I have umbrellas."

Secret Bear smiled and said, "And the secret about clouds is that they all have silver linings."

"What do you mean?"
asked Grumpy Bear.

"I mean something good will come of the rain," said Secret Bear. "Just wait and see!" 15

"And there it is!" said Cheer Bear.

"A beautiful rainbow
to ride down to our picnic!

Whee!"

Laughing, the Care Bears landed in a heap at Share Bear's feet.

"What's the matter?" Cheer Bear asked.

18

"I brought five sunshine bars and five rainbow bars, but they all broke in two," said Share Bear, sighing.

"What terrible luck," grumbled Grumpy Bear.

"Remember, every cloud has a **silver lining**," Secret Bear said.

"That's right!" exclaimed Funshine Bear.
"Now we can each taste both treats!"

"Come with us to the picnic, Bedtime Bear!"
said Cheer Bear.

"I can't. I lost my starry nightcap, and I have to find it," Bedtime Bear replied.

"Oh dear, another problem," said Grumpy Bear.
"Remember the silver lining," said Secret Bear, smiling. "We just have to look for it."

"And for Bedtime Bear's missing
cap!" Best Friend Bear added.

"Look, Share Bear found my missing picnic blanket!" Cheer Bear said.

"That's lucky for us," said Secret Bear.

"We never would have found the blanket
if Bedtime Bear hadn't lost his nightcap."

"But we still
haven't found it," said
Bedtime Bear.

SWEET
DREAMS

"There it is!"

shouted Secret Bear.
"It was in my favorite napping
spot," said Bedtime Bear.

"This is also a perfect spot for a picnic!" Cheer Bear added.

"Now let's have some fun!"
Funshine Bear shouted.

"Not yet," said Secret Bear.
"Love-a-lot Bear, Wish Bear, and
Bashful Heart Bear aren't here yet."

"What's the **silver lining** in that?" wondered Grumpy Bear.

"Sorry we're late!" said Wish Bear.

"We were taking time to fill the picnic basket with everyone's favorites," said Love-a-lot Bear.

"And making enough rainbow punch for everyone," said Bashful Heart Bear.

"All you have to do is look for it!" said Secret Bear.

"And best of all, this one is delicious!"

Picnic

Do you ever have grumpy days like Grumpy Bear?

❤ What helps to cheer you up?
❤ Do you have someone special who makes you feel better?

A lot of things went wrong with the Care Bears' picnic.

- ♥ Have your plans ever been ruined?
- ♥ What did you do?

Grumpy Bear learned to look for the silver lining.

- ♥ What does that mean?
- ♥ How can you look for the silver lining when something goes wrong?

Bashful Heart Bear

Cheer Bear

Share Bear

Bedtime Bear

Funshine Bear